Under Siege

Steve Barlow and Steve Skidmore ■ Jonatronix

OXFORD
UNIVERSITY PRESS

Chapter 1 – Knight school

Tiger looked up at the flags fluttering from the battlements of the castle. *This is going to be brilliant!* he thought.

Tiger and his friends stood on the wooden drawbridge that crossed the moat. They gazed up at the high stone towers.

"Those walls look as if they could keep an army out!" said Tiger.

Ant chuckled. "That was the idea!"

They went through the gatehouse and into the castle yard. Ant checked his guidebook. "This yard is called the bailey." He pointed to the great stone building on the opposite side of the castle. "And that's the keep."

"If we go in there, perhaps it will *keep* Dr X and his X-bots away from us," said Cat.

Max laughed. "We're far away from NASTI. Dr X won't be able to find us here."

Greenville Castle map

curtain wall

towers

bailey

gatehouse

moat

keep

great hall

Ant looked up from his guidebook. A short, stout jester and a tall minstrel caught his attention.

"Great! Medieval entertainment," he chuckled.

"I say, I say, I say!" the jester shouted. "Knock, knock."

The minstrel stopped playing. "Who's there?"

"Jester," said the jester.

"Jester who?" asked the minstrel.

"Jester minute," chuckled the jester, "I've left the kettle on …"

Cat pulled a face. "They're not very good."
Something was tugging at the back of her mind. Had
she seen them before somewhere?

"Good day, friends!" A man wearing a tunic gave
the children a sweeping bow. "Wouldst thou join our
knight school?"

Tiger stared at him. "Huh?"

"It's a Living History day," Ant reminded him.
"They have re-enactors to show us how people lived
in the past."

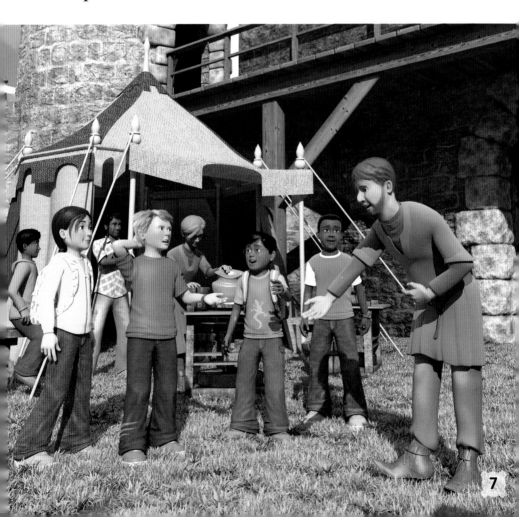

They followed the man into the keep and went up some stone steps to a large room. The man pushed open the heavy door. "This is the great hall," he said.

The hall was full of fantastic displays. There was so much to look at.

In the middle of the room was a model of the castle. Ant's eyes glowed as he stared at it. "Excellent! It's just like the real castle, down to the last detail!"

Tiger noticed something else. "Look! We can try on the armour!"

All around the hall an army of small knights was working in groups.

"What are they doing?" asked Cat.

"They're making model siege engines," said the re-enactor. "There's a competition to see who can build the best one."

"What's a siege engine?" Tiger asked Ant, as he tried on a helmet.

"It's a machine for throwing rocks," Ant told him. "Armies used them to break down castle walls."

"Wilt thou enter our competition?" asked the re-enactor.

Tiger rubbed his hands in glee. A machine for breaking things? *Brilliant!* "You bet we will!"

Chapter 2 – Trapped!

Max put the finishing touches to his and Cat's siege engine and wiped his brow. He took off his armour. "This is hard work," he said. "I need an ice cream."

Ant licked his lips. "Great idea." He put down his helmet and followed Max through the door.

Cat and Tiger looked up. The other model-makers and the re-enactor had already finished and left the room. Cat and Tiger were alone.

Tiger grinned. "I had Ant on my team. I bet our machine's better than yours."

"I bet it's not," said Cat.

"Let's find out," said Tiger. He pointed to a pile of small pebbles beside the siege engines. "Let's see which one throws the furthest."

"You're on!" said Cat. "Let's shrink. Then it'll be more fun!"

They turned the dials on their watches. They pushed the X and …

Cat and Tiger climbed on to the table. They worked hard to wind back their engines' throwing arms. The pebbles were now the size of boulders and very heavy.

Cat and Tiger didn't notice the minstrel and the jester they had seen earlier creep into the room. The minstrel and jester tiptoed towards the model castle, making 'shushing' signals to each other.

The minstrel put down his lute. In the twinkling of an eye, he picked up a glass dome from one of the displays and dropped it over the children.

Cat and Tiger were trapped!

Cat stared up at their captors in horror. "I know those two!" she cried. "I remember now! I saw them at NASTI! They're Dr X's henchmen!"

Tiger gulped. "You're right – and they've got us just where they want us!"

Chapter 3 – Don't move!

Plug was delighted. "Dr X is going to be really pleased with us!"

"I'll ring him now." Socket reached for his phone.

However, before he could make the call, there was the sound of voices outside the door. Socket picked up his lute.

"… and this is the great hall." The voice belonged to a stern-looking lady wearing glasses and a badge that said 'Guide'.

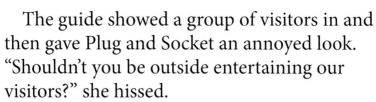

The guide showed a group of visitors in and then gave Plug and Socket an annoyed look. "Shouldn't you be outside entertaining our visitors?" she hissed.

"Oh right," said Plug, remembering he was supposed to be a jester. "I say, I say, I say!" he burbled. "What do you call a flea in a metal suit?"

"I don't know," said Socket.

"A bite in shining armour!" answered Plug.

The guide groaned. "Is that the best you can do? It's terrible! Just go outside and jingle your bells or something."

Plug and Socket went out through the door. They glanced back anxiously at the glass dome covering their prisoners.

"Now," she said, "if you look at the model of the castle, you can see that …" She pointed. "Oh, look. Our young visitors have been busy making model siege engines! They've even put a couple of model knights beside them."

Her voice boomed around inside the glass cover. Tiger gave Cat a horrified look. "They think we're models!" he hissed as the visitors crowded around for a closer look.

"I know!" whispered Cat.

"What do we do?" moaned Tiger.

"Nothing! We'll just have to wait for the visitors to go. Keep quiet – and whatever you do, don't move!"

Chapter 4 – Hide and seek

Meanwhile …

Max crunched up the last of his ice cream cone and looked around.

"Where are Cat and Tiger?" he asked.

"I don't know," said Ant, who was still enjoying his ice cream. "I thought they'd be finished by now."

The castle was very crowded. Lots of visitors were walking between the coloured tents dotted around the castle yard. Some of the tents were serving refreshments. Others had displays of crafts or cookery demonstrations. In one, an armourer was making chain mail.

Max and Ant felt like they'd travelled back in time. They hurried from tent to tent trying to spot their friends. There was no sign of Cat and Tiger anywhere.

Max was worried. "How are we going to find them with all these people about?"

"Don't worry," said Ant. "It's not as if they're in any danger from Dr X. Maybe they're still in the great hall."

"We'd better check." Max led the way to the keep.

The great hall was full of visitors. Most of them were gathered around the model of the castle. A guide was talking to them. "Of course, castle walls were very strong, so siege engines had to be big and powerful …"

Max looked around. "I can't see Cat and Tiger," he said.

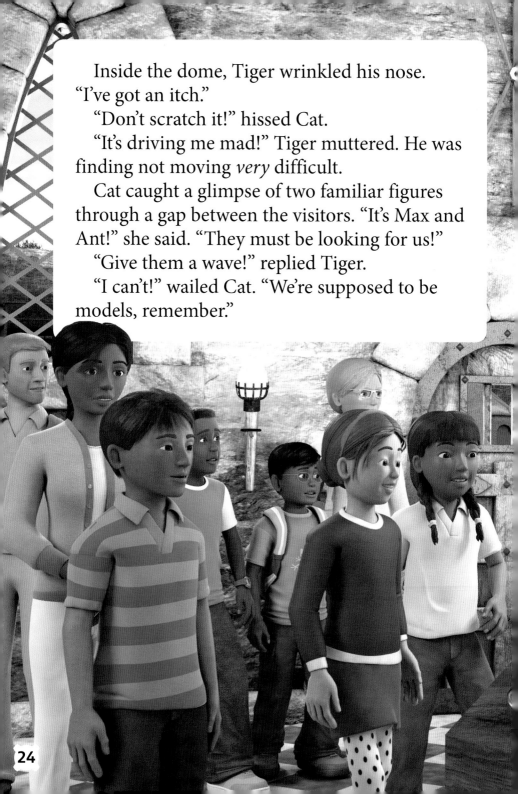

Inside the dome, Tiger wrinkled his nose. "I've got an itch."

"Don't scratch it!" hissed Cat.

"It's driving me mad!" Tiger muttered. He was finding not moving *very* difficult.

Cat caught a glimpse of two familiar figures through a gap between the visitors. "It's Max and Ant!" she said. "They must be looking for us!"

"Give them a wave!" replied Tiger.

"I can't!" wailed Cat. "We're supposed to be models, remember."

The guide's voice boomed around the glass dome. "Now, if you will follow me, a tournament is about to start in the castle yard."

"They must have gone to the tournament," Ant whispered to Max.

Max nodded and they followed the guide out with the rest of the visitors. Tiger slumped in relief. "Thank goodness! We can move again."

"Max and Ant have gone!" Cat groaned.

"Don't worry," said Tiger. "They'll come back."

Chapter 5 – Fire!

Cat's watch could track her friends. She looked at it now. "They're not coming back – they're going away! What if Dr X's henchmen come back?" Cat gazed wildly at the walls of their glass prison. "We have to get out of here!"

Tiger shrugged helplessly. "Yes, but how? If we grow, the glass dome will shatter. It's too dangerous!"

Cat thought hard for a moment. "The siege engines!" she exclaimed.

Tiger stared at her. "What about them?"

"Why don't we fire pebbles at the dome? We can break it and get out!"

"That's a brilliant idea!" Tiger immediately began rolling a pebble towards his siege engine.

Cat fired first. Her pebble soared through the air. It hit the dome with a loud crack but the dome didn't break.

Then Tiger fired. His shot hit the dome higher up. There was a splintering noise and a crack appeared in the glass.

Tiger gave a whoop but Cat shook her head. "It still hasn't broken! We'll have to fire again – together, this time!"

They loaded the siege engines again. It was hard work. Cat and Tiger were very hot and tired when they had finished.

"Ready?" asked Tiger.

Cat wasn't listening. She was gazing in horror at the door. It was creaking open …

"Dr X's henchmen are coming back!" yelled Cat. "It's now or never! One … two … three!"

The pebbles sailed through the air together. They crashed into the dome. A section of glass shattered and fell away just as Plug and Socket burst into the great hall.

"Run!" yelled Cat and Tiger together.

Chapter 6 – Escape

Plug and Socket stared in horror at the broken dome and the fleeing figures of their prisoners.

"I say, I say, I say! They're escaping!" howled Plug.

"Grab them!" roared Socket.

Plug and Socket dived towards the children. Plug tripped over his jester's stick. Socket bumped into Plug and fell on his lute. They ended up in a tangle on the floor.

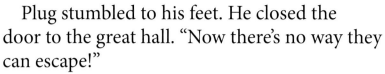

Plug stumbled to his feet. He closed the door to the great hall. "Now there's no way they can escape!"

"Where did they go?" asked Socket.

"They must be hiding in the model castle somewhere," said Plug. They stared at the model, trying to peer through the tiny doors.

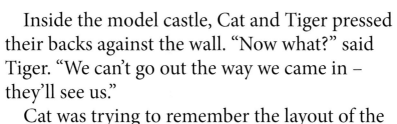

Inside the model castle, Cat and Tiger pressed their backs against the wall. "Now what?" said Tiger. "We can't go out the way we came in – they'll see us."

Cat was trying to remember the layout of the model. "Maybe we won't have to. There was a small door at the back of the model keep. If we find it, we can sneak out without them noticing."

Tiger brightened. "It's worth a try."

They crept through the model until they found the door. Cat opened it a crack and looked out. Dr X's men were nowhere to be seen. As she'd expected, they were at the other end of the model, watching the gatehouse.

Cat opened the door wider. "Come on," she whispered. Tiger followed her through the door. Stealthily, they crept away from the model.

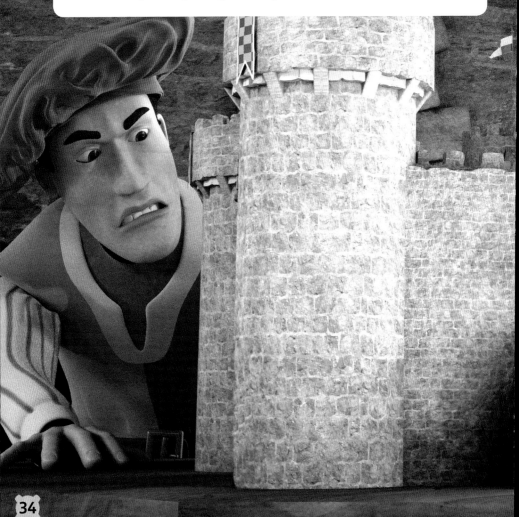

"I say, I say, I say! There they are!"
Cat gave a gasp of horror. They had
been spotted!

Luckily, Plug and Socket tripped over the jester's stick and lute *again!*

Plug was lying flat on his back just beside the table. Cat and Tiger jumped off the table and bounced off his stomach.

"Ow!" yelped Plug.

"Great!" chuckled Tiger. "A soft landing!"

Tiger grabbed Cat's arm and pointed at a door in the corner of the room. "Look – there's a gap underneath! We can squeeze through it."

They reached the door and rolled underneath it before Dr X's men could catch them.

The door handle above them rattled furiously. It was locked. Cat gave a sigh of relief. "We're safe!"

Chapter 7 – A leap in the dark

Tiger picked himself up and looked around. "Safe, maybe – but this room doesn't go anywhere. It's a dead end!"

Cat and Tiger grew back to normal size and looked around.

"What is this place?" asked Tiger.

Cat giggled. "I know where we are – we're in the garderobe."

"What's that?" asked Tiger.

"A medieval loo." Cat pointed. "That hole leads straight down to the moat."

Tiger caught on. "So if you needed the toilet, you'd sit there and …" He wrinkled his nose. "That's disgusting."

"It could be a way out," said Cat thoughtfully.

Tiger stared at her. "What? Down a loo? Yeuch! Anyway, we'd never get through that hole."

"We could shrink again."

"All right, but then what? It's too far to jump and too hard to climb down." (*And probably really smelly*, Tiger thought to himself.)

"I know!" Cat rummaged in her backpack.

"Our micro-copter!" exclaimed Tiger. "I didn't know you'd brought it."

"I just thought it might come in useful."

"Will it carry both of us?" asked Tiger anxiously.

Just then, the door shuddered. Dr X's men were trying to force their way in!

"I think we'd better find out!" said Cat.

Cat put the micro-copter down beside the hole. Then she and Tiger pressed the buttons on their watches and shrank.

Cat and Tiger each held on to one of the straps of the micro-copter. Tiger started the motor. The door shuddered again.

"Let's go!" Tiger shouted.

Cat and Tiger jumped into the hole.

To Tiger's relief, the chute they were falling down wasn't very smelly at all. It soon came to an end and they burst out into the open air.

Cat looked down and gasped. "Pull the throttle now or we'll fall into the moat!"

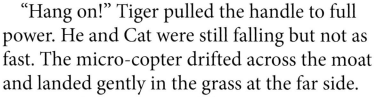

"Hang on!" Tiger pulled the handle to full power. He and Cat were still falling but not as fast. The micro-copter drifted across the moat and landed gently in the grass at the far side.

Cat and Tiger let go of the straps.

Cat took her helmet off and wiped the sweat from her brow. "That was a narrow escape!"

Tiger looked around. "I wonder where the others are?"

Chapter 8 – Foiled again!

Cat and Tiger found their friends watching the knights' tournament.

"There you are, at last!" said Max.

Ant grinned. "I told you we'd only have to wait here and they'd turn up eventually."

"Where did you disappear to?" demanded Max.

Tiger eagerly told them all about Dr X's henchmen.

"I'm glad we made those siege engines!" said Ant.

"Ours worked the best," Tiger told him.

"No it didn't!" said Cat crossly.

"Yes it did. It was the first one to crack the glass …"

"Anyway," said Max. "I bet Dr X is thinking up another plan right now. We'll need to be on our guard."

Cat giggled. "Speaking of guards – I'd love to see their faces when they break down the door to the garderobe!"

CRASH! Plug and Socket had finally managed to break open the garderobe door. They stumbled into the tiny room and stared around in dismay.

"I say, I say, I say!" said Plug. "They've gone!"

"Will you stop saying, *I say, I say, I say!*" snapped Socket. He reached for his phone. "The boss isn't going to like this …"

He was right. Dr X wasn't pleased at all.

"You told me you had them trapped!" he shouted. Socket looked sheepish. "Sorry, boss."

"And now you've let them escape down some old lavatory. I'll have you cleaning out the NASTI loos for a month for your stupidity!"

"But, Boss," objected Plug, "you already make us clean out the loos …"

Dr X wasn't listening. An evil grin spread over his face. "All is not lost. I have another plan, one those kids will never see coming …"

Find out more ...

Find out what
happens next, read
Dungeon Danger.

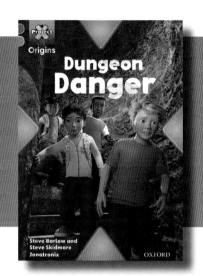